DATE			
MAY 2 6		KZ. H 2	FEB 7
	NOV 8		
Eva Z. Alvarez			
	APR 2		
			FEB 1
	JUN 3		NOV 1
		SSS	FEB 2

398.2   Werth, Kurt
WER
          Molly and the giant

                                    $5

MOLLY
AND THE GIANT

By Kurt Werth And Mabel Watts

Illustrated By Kurt Werth

PARENTS' MAGAZINE PRESS / NEW YORK

Text Copyright © 1973 by Kurt Werth and Mabel Watts
Illustrations Copyright © 1973 by Kurt Werth
All rights reserved
Printed in the United States of America

Library of Congress Cataloging in Publication Data
Werth, Kurt.
    Molly and the giant.
    SUMMARY: At the expense of the giant, brave, smart
Molly seeks and finds fortune for herself and her two
timid sisters.
    [1. Fairy tales. 2. Folklore—Great Britain]
I. Watts, Mabel, joint author. II Title.
PZ8.W493Mo   398.2'1'09415   72-6076
ISBN 0-8193-0638-X   ISBN 0-8193-0639-8 (lib. ed.)

MOLLY AND THE GIANT

Once upon a time in a poor Irish cottage, there lived a girl named Molly O'Shea. She was beautiful as a bog flower, brave as a lion, and smart as a treeful of owls.

Aye, and a good thing it was, for her two older sisters were shy as violets and timid as hares.

"Molly, come here," said her father one day, when the hens wouldn't lay, the pigs had the pip, and potatoes were scarce as feathers on a frog. "Molly, my dear," he said, "'twould be best, I'm thinking, if you and your sisters left this poor little cottage to seek your fortunes elsewhere."

"We'll be after going this very day," said Molly, cheerfully as she could. "We'll do what we have to do, and you'll not be hearing from us again till our fortunes are found and our futures are bright!"

The three sisters walked a long weary way with-
out even stopping. And at the end of the day they
came to a hidden house in a tangled woods. Finding
the door ajar, they walked right in and called,
"Hullooo!"

"Have you no sense at all," asked the woman
who lived there, "to be entering the house of my husband, the giant?"

"Giant or no," said Molly, "being tired and hungry, we are willing to take our chances, even if it should be the end of us."

"Then stay, and welcome," said the giant's wife. "And may Heaven protect you from whatever may come!" She sat them down by a blazing fire and brought them plates of Irish stew.

Troth, and they had no more than taken a bite when the giant himself came blundering in. "Bedad," he said, as he filled his plate, "if there's anything better than Irish stew, 'tis a girl in a pot with parsley sauce!"

While the giant ate in his terrible way, his wife
led the sisters upstairs to a wide feather bed where
three giant children lay sleeping. "Where there's
room for three, there's room for six!" she said.
"Good night, my dears, and pleasant dreams."

Sure, and it wasn't long before the giant came
clumping up the stairs, with three chains of gold in
his one hand and three braids of straw in the other.

Clumsily, he placed the chains of gold around the
necks of his children. "The better to know my own
in the dark!" he said. "And you, my fair mavour-
neens, shall wear these braids of straw!"

"The better to find his midnight supper," Molly told her sisters the moment he was gone. Och an*ee*! And it didn't take her long to change those necklaces! "Straw for the giant's children," she whispered. "Gold for us."

Down the stairs and out the door they crept, the three of them. They made their way through thicket and bramble in the stormy, desperate weather till they reached the castle of the king.

When the guard saw the three golden necklaces shining in the morning, he opened up the gates and invited them in. "Three princesses in a row," he said, "all come to see the King of Erin!"

Three in a row, the sisters curtsied low before the king. "Ahh," he said, "the necklaces you wear were stolen from this very castle many long years ago!"

Och an*ee*! And though Molly looked like something the cat might drag in after a wild and stormy night on the peat bog, she was soon telling the king how she and her sisters happened to be wearing them.

She was about to rest her feet and eat a buttered crumpet, when the king said, "A girl like you could be very helpful!"

"Faith," said Molly, "and how can a girl so poor help a king so rich?"

"She can go back to the house of the giant and fetch me his sword," said the king. "The sword he stole from this very castle many long years ago.

"Do this for me," he went on, "and it's your eldest sister can have my eldest son in marriage and a castle of their own to live in."

"I'll be after doing my best, even if it should be the end of me," said Molly, not wanting to fall from the king's good graces.

"Then be smart. Be brave. And be *off*!" said the king.

Back at the hidden house, Molly found the giant asleep in his bed, the whole of him, with his sword on the wall overhead. 'Twill be a ticklish job altogether, she thought. But up she climbed onto the bed. Then, just as she was reaching and stretching, and doing right bravely, down crashed the sword with a klunk and a clatter.

Wakened by the noise, the giant burst from his bed and reached for Molly's hair. "So it's yourself again," he roared, "plague that you are!"

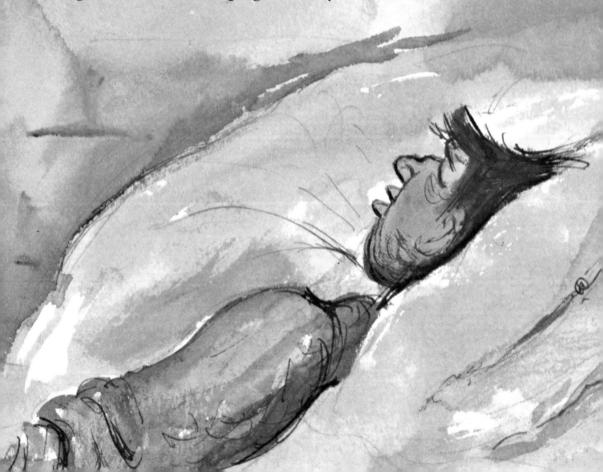

Breathless with fear, Molly slipped through his fingers and ran with the sword. Over hump and hollow she dashed, with the shadow of the giant forever before her.

Troth, and if she hadn't reached the Bridge of True Love's Hair in the nick of time—as she did—the giant would surely have caught her, the king would never have recovered his sword, and Molly's eldest sister would never have married the king's eldest son.

Och an*ee*! Molly had never seen such grandeur in all her life. But just as she was catching her breath, resting her feet, and eating her fill at the royal banquet, the king took her aside.

"Recovering my sword was indeed great and glorious," he said. "But what I want more than that is the bag of gold that the giant stole from this very castle—ten years ago come Christmas.

"Bring me that gold," said he, "and it's your second sister can have my second son in marriage and a castle of their own to live in."

"I'll be after doing my best," said Molly, "though my feet are tired, my legs are hurting, and the giant is about to kill me!"

"This bottle of wine will suit him fine," said the king, as Molly set out on her second journey.

In the hidden house in the tangled woods sat the terrible giant, right in the window. Drinking his tea from a bucket, he was, with the bag of gold beside him. While his back was turned, Molly set the bottle of wine on the table, and it was just to the giant's taste.

"'Tis better than tea," said he. And the more he drank, the sillier he became. Giddy as a goose, he stuffed the bag of gold under his pillow and fell fast asleep with his head on top of it.

Molly tugged at this corner and that, trying to get the bag. And with every tug and pull, the giant tossed and turned in his sleep, all seven hundred pounds of him.

Troth, and he never woke up till the bag of gold was walking across the floor.

"I am going for a stroll," said the voice beneath the bag. "Stay right where you are, and I'll soon be back!"

"Imagine that," said the giant drowsily. "My bag of gold is walking and talking, which is queer altogether."

"'Tis Molly O'Shea that's walking and talking," said the giant's wife. Faith, and she could have bitten off her tongue for saying it and thereby giving poor Molly away.

The giant tumbled out of bed. "She's getting away with my gold!" he roared. And once again the chase began.

Troth, and if she hadn't reached the Bridge of True Love's Hair in the nick of time—as she did— the giant would surely have caught her, the king would never have recovered his bagful of gold, and Molly's second sister would never have married the king's second son.

Aye, Molly had never seen such pomp and splendor in all her life. But once the dancing, the feasting and the merriment were over, the king crooked his finger at Molly and said, "Come!"

What *more* could the King of Erin possibly want?

"What I want now," said the king, in answer to Molly's unspoken question, "is the ring you'll find on the giant's thumb.

"Fetch me that ring," said he, "and it's yourself can have my youngest son in marriage, and your very own castle besides."

"Wait!" said the king's youngest son, as Molly started out. "Inside this locket is something to help you when you need it most."

Now the king's youngest son was a handsome, dashing lad, and Molly was fair enchanted. For him she would do just about anything!

With the locket around her neck, the promise of a prince, and a piece of wedding cake in her pocket, Molly put her best foot forward—and there was no turning back.

In the hidden house in the tangled woods, Molly found the giant sprawled on his bed, snoring and snorting, with the ring on his thumb. Molly opened the locket, and sure it was full of goose grease. With the help of the grease, 'twas easy as pie. A twist, a turn, and off came the ring.

But just as Molly was fastening it inside her pocket with a safety pin so she wouldn't be losing it, the giant awoke.

"Bedad and begorrah!" he yelled, as he snatched her up in his hand. "If I had done to you what you have done to me, what then would my punishment be?"

Being smart as a treeful of owls, Molly carefully thought out her answer. "I would bundle you into a sack," she said at last, "with a dog and a cat, a needle and thread, and a sharp pair of scissors. Aye, then I'd hang the sack on the wall and beat you smartly with a stick."

"And that," said the giant, "is exactly what your punishment shall be!"

After he'd put Molly into a sack with a dog and a cat, a needle and thread, and a sharp pair of scissors, and hung it on the wall, he said, "Now for a stick!"

While the giant was out in the tangled woods, looking for the proper stick, Molly cut a hole in the sack with the scissors. Out she jumped, and the dog and the cat, too. They couldn't get away fast enough.

Molly neatly mended the sack with the needle and thread, and filled it full of oatmeal so it would look fat and bumpy as before. This was no sooner done when the giant returned with the stick—the biggest, thickest stick in all Ireland.

Molly hid behind a door, brave as ever but twice as scared.

"Bedad!" said the giant. "I'll give that girl a clouting she'll never forget. Take *that*, Molly O'Shea," he said, full of meanness and full of glee. "And *that*. And *that*. And *that*!"

So busy was the giant clouting the sack—and so sure Molly was in it—that he couldn't believe his eyes when he saw her tumbling out through the window.

"You'll be the death of me yet!" he raged, and he clumped after her, waving his stick.

Troth, and if Molly hadn't reached the Bridge of True Love's Hair in the nick of time—for which she was ten times thankful—the giant would surely have caught her, the king would never have recovered his ring, and Molly would never have married the king's youngest son . . . which she did!

Dizzy with joy, she gave him her promise true, just like a proper princess, and there was great rejoicing.

Aye, with her fortune found and her future bright, Molly went with her husband to a castle of their own, where they lived happily ever after.

Kurt Werth was born in Leipzig, Germany, and always wanted to be an artist, despite the misgivings of his parents. After graduation from the State Academy for Graphic Arts in Leipzig, he began a career as an illustrator of books and satirical magazines. However, he and his actress wife were forced to leave Germany during the Nazi regime. Mr. Werth started over again in New York City, first with political cartoons, illustrating textbooks, and at last children's books, illustrating over 75, mostly for the 6-to-12 age group. He found *Molly and the Giant*—his first book for Parents'—in an old collection of Irish folktales.

Mabel Watts has many children's books to her credit, not to mention the countless stories she has contributed to *Humpty Dumpty's Magazine* and other magazines for children. She is the author of *The Boy Who Listened to Everyone, Henrietta and the Hat, The King and the Whirlybird, The Story of Zachary Zween* and *While the Horses Galloped to London,* all published by Parents' Magazine Press. Born in England, Mrs. Watts has made California her home for many years.